DECK THE HALLS AND MURDER

A Fiona Fleming Cozy Novella

PATTI LARSEN

Cover design by Christina Gaudet
www.castlekeepcreations.com

Thanks, Kirstin!

ISBN-13: 978-1-998948-47-5

CHAPTER ONE

I shifted the shining red ornament in favor of the crocheted white angel with the gold halo and stepped back, eyeing the difference. Sighed and put the decorations back the way they'd been, instead unclipping the cord of the light string and moving the row of colored bulbs down just a smidge before smiling, satisfied.

The tree looked amazing, I had to say, glowing star at the top alight with new, white bulbs, the evergreen dominating the sitting room shining out the window and casting a lovely, multi-colored festive wash over the grass in the front yard. Yes, grass. No snow, not yet, but I had hopes for Christmas, a mere week away.

This was the Green Mountains of Vermont, after

all. While unseasonably warm so far, a storm could blow in at any moment and blanket my picturesque little hometown in a thick bed of white that would take months to melt.

A girl could dream, right?

I hummed along to a popular carol playing from the speakers in the dining room as I exited into the foyer and checked my computer for late arrivals. From the looks of things all of my guests were present and accounted for, which meant the plans I had with Daisy for tonight were a go after all. The scent of evergreen and cinnamon dominated the entry of my bed and breakfast, sweeping banister to the second floor wound with real boughs—Mom insisted and I agreed wholeheartedly with her trek into the woods dragging Dad along for muscle—and the gorgeous, antique decorations my Grandmother Iris so carefully preserved and used year after year.

Last year had been a whirlwind and while I'd done some adornment, I hadn't had time to sort through all the boxes of delights she'd left me along with her beautiful B&B. This year, I took the time, recruiting Mom and Daisy to assist and, a day spent oohing and ahhing and reminiscing over old treasures ended in the truly stunning and merry look we'd achieved.

From the sleigh bells hanging from the front door ready to chime their cheer at every opening to the holiday-themed tablecloths and napkins, to the Christmas centerpieces and glass angels and Christmas trees set about in every room, Petunia's had been transformed into its own little winter wonderland.

And I couldn't have been happier about it.

I beamed down at the fat fawn pug sitting at my feet, her own decorative red bandana with the fur lining giving her that happy holidays panache I had already photographed and posted on social media ad nauseum because, oh my goodness, wasn't she just the cutest? While I'd always loved Christmas, this year just felt... different. Maybe it was how settled I felt in Reading finally, how happy and confident in my place here, how comfortable running my bed and breakfast. Whatever the reason, this holiday season was bound to be amazing, and I couldn't wait for the big day and Ho Ho Ho.

Don't tease a girl for being thirty going on twelve.

I bolded the note I'd left for the staff NOT to book the four days I'd marked off for any reason, just in case. As of December 23rd until the 27th, Petunia's was all mine. Mom and Dad and Day were even coming for the holidays, to stay over, a little mini-vacation for all of us. My mouth watered at the thought of Mom's amazing turkey dinner, her epic stuffing.

Best. Christmas. Ever.

And just the beginning.

The front door opened right on time with that lovely ringing I was sure I'd be sick of before Christmas was over. Daisy swept through, looking all kinds of cheery in her red wool flare coat and matching mittens, an adorable Santa hat perched on her dark blonde curls, those gray eyes sparkling with delight and her beautiful face a wreath of smiles.

"Are you ready?" She bent to scratch Petunia behind the ears when my pug waddled to her side looking for attention.

Was I. "All set," I said, fetching my coat, wishing I'd thought to get a hat of my own, feeling a bit drab in my long, black coat and boots. Even as Day, beaming a smile, whipped out a second hat from inside her own and handed it to me before liberating two strings of lights from her pocket, clicking the buttons on the necklaces of bulbs so they flashed into life.

"I couldn't resist," she giggled while I laughed and hugged her.

"This," I said, slipping the garland of lights over my jacket, tugging the hat firmly over my red hair, "is only one reason I love you so much."

Daisy dimpled while I slipped Petunia into her harness. The door to the kitchen swung open, April—or Andy? Hmmm… Ashley?—waving at me as we exited the B&B for the fun ahead.

"I'm just so happy you're home." She linked arms with me, Petunia leading us across the street as if knowing exactly where we were going and why. More likely, she thought we were heading to Sammy's Coffee for a donut hole, but she was waddling in the right direction, so I let her have her head as we strolled. "This has been the most amazing eighteen months."

"Aside from the murders, you mean." I winked at

her, laughed. "Day, I agree." I inhaled the crisp air that surely felt like snow, right? "This is going to be an amazing year. I just know it."

Oh, Fleming. I had to learn to be careful what I said. The Universe was always listening. Especially knowing said Universe had a rather interesting sense of humor.

I brushed off the trepidation I'd created in my own mind and chose to enjoy the evening with my best friend. What was the worst that could happen?

Fee. *Seriously.*

CHAPTER TWO

The center of the massive metropolitan downtown (snort) that was Reading's Main Street was already lined with residents, many faces I recognized blending together into a sea of smiling humanity topped in many cases in antlers, Santa and elf hats, the jingle of bells and flashing of personal light strings evidence Daisy hadn't been the only one unable to resist the call of the festive.

I tucked in closer to my bestie, shortening Petunia's leash to keep her out from underfoot, though from the snuffling she did on the pavement, the way the odd child turned to squeal and hug her and stuff something clandestine and definitely not on her diet into her eager mouth, made me groan over the epic farting I'd be dealing with all night and likely well into tomorrow. I loved my adopted pug, the fourth in a long line of Petunias named for the very B&B I managed, but if the guests and everyone else who thought she was adorable (she was, darn it, part of the problem) didn't stop feeding her various treats that fired up her intestines to tragic result, I wasn't going to survive her. Being gassed at two in the morning was getting old.

"Look, there are your folks." Daisy tugged on me, waving and beaming at Mom and Dad where the former sheriff of these here parts and the retired principal who knew everyone by name stood near the corner of Main and Poplar. Dad towered over my petite mother, as usual, though I looked enough like her with her heavy red hair and blue eyes I knew I'd age gracefully, ever so grateful for that fact. I did, however, welcome some of Dad's height, though my 5'7" wasn't exactly Amazonian. Still, at least that meant I didn't have to ask anyone to reach for things on high shelves or feel intimidated by those bigger than myself.

Not that Lucy Fleming was intimidated by anyone. If anything, the small, beautiful redhead who hugged me when I joined them had that air of someone who could take on the whole world and never flinch.

As for the stoic and yet kind male side of the Fleming duo, his own eyes sparkled, Dad's grin almost boyish as he let me go before hugging Daisy and then crouching to ruffle Petunia's ears.

"I do wish it had snowed," Mom said, hands

clasped in front of her tucked into velvety soft gloves, her hair held back behind her own Santa hat. Dad's reindeer antlers flashed, the tiny embedded bulbs sure to give me a headache if I looked at him for too long, though I had to admit, the fact Mom talked him into them made me giggle.

I wrinkled my nose at my mother, and though I'd had the exact same thought earlier, shrugged. "It's winter in Vermont, Mom," I said.

"It'll snow when it snows." Dad finished that line, one that I was positive every single person in Reading had uttered at one point or another since the dawn of freaking time.

Daisy sighed with complete contentment. "At least the parade won't be held up," she said. Waved across the street with that same enthusiasm she showed for everyone she met. While my gaze followed her excitement and I caught myself grinning and waving, too. Deputy Jill Wagner waved back, a single motion of her wrist, clearly on duty if her uniform was any indication. Never mind that, even as I smiled at her, my gaze drifted sideways to the tall, handsome man who joined her, his dark curls covered in a knitted cap instead of the cowboy hat he liked to wear, blue eyes lifting to meet mine from the opposite corner.

I know my smile shifted. I couldn't help it. Not because I wanted it to. Sheriff Crew Turner had that effect on me. The mishmash of emotions that ranged from irritated frustration to hormonal va-va-va-voom never failed to make interactions with Captain

Handsompants about as awkward as possible.

Didn't help I had a bad habit of solving his murder cases for him, either. Something he was always very careful to point out in that annoyingly calm and confident way of his. That was until I stirred his temper, his very long and patient fuse, to the point the under-eye tic showed up along with that vein that stood out on his forehead.

Well, you know what? I was in a great mood and decided to let bygones be bygones. Waved and grinned at him, too, and, to my surprise, caught the slow and sexy (dear god, so sexy) smile in return as he mimicked Jill's single gesture in return.

Friends, then. Or, at least, not enemies. I had no illusions. Things had been rather tense since Halloween and the death of Sadie Hatch. While I hadn't set out to yet again poke my nose in where it wasn't wanted and failed to mind my own business (yes, that was Crew's voice you just heard saying those things), I just couldn't seem to follow through. Not my fault people brought me clues and information and dumped things in my lap that ended in cases being solved though, right?

There was only one thing that could shift my mood (okay, two, but the likelihood a dead body was going to drop out of the sky was slim to none, so let's narrow things down, shall we?) to the worse and that particular thing chose that particular moment to do his particular brand of yuck and make himself known.

By stopping next to me, hocking up a nice load

and spitting on the ground next to my boot. I looked up—barely—into those eyes empty of anything but contempt and baseless judgment and did my best not to punch my truly horrendous cousin Robert in the face. Since he was a deputy after all. Hitting him might get me arrested. Might, because, truth be told, I knew the sheriff didn't like him either and would likely give me a pat on the back behind closed doors for a job well done.

"You make sure to run home to bed after this, Fanny," Robert sneered. "Little girls out past their bedtime are just asking for trouble."

Okay, there was nothing not gross about Robert Carlisle, but that comment? Went further even than he and his 70's porn star mustache had ever gone before. I think he knew it, too, because he backed off, shooting me with his thumb and index finger before carrying on to torment other people for no good reason.

So tempting to follow him down a dark alley and do all of Reading a permanent favor.

Instead, I chose the high road and, when he passed the stand as a reminder of its presence, a cup of hot chocolate.

I left Petunia with Daisy and headed for the cart, standing in line for my turn, hugging myself against the chill though my heart was full. This was the first time I'd get to see the Reading Christmas Parade since I was a teenager, my ten years in New York City kind of a blur of college, working and being cheated on by my ex-boyfriend. Yes, the holidays in

Manhattan were epic, from the tree in Rockefeller Square to ice-skating in Central Park, how the big retailers went all out with decorations in the stores not to mention the lights everywhere courtesy of the city. But there was something so deliciously lovely about the more economical—but no less enthusiastic—decorations that adorned my beloved hometown, an air of not just festivities but of community and caring during the holiday season that I'd missed out on for a long time.

Had taken for granted and wished away. Until I came home. Realized what I'd given up. Decided to embrace and, to my internal delight, knew I'd never turn my back on again.

I caught sight of Mayor Olivia Walker near the tall set of red curtains that had been set up in front of town hall, just a block away. She was impossible to miss, even from a distance. With her smooth, black bob tucked into a white fur hat and her entire body decked out in white wool, she snapped commands I caught the tail ends of despite the fact the local high school band was tuning up nearby and drowned out most of what she had to say.

No doubt the later parade date and town tree reveal was part of some master plan she had to increase Reading's tourist trade since that was all she seemed to think about. Not complaining or anything, but I wished, for once, she'd stop and enjoy what she created. As for me, unlike my first year back when I still felt disjointed and rather out of place, struggling to sort out who I was and why I'd come home, this year I chose to make the very most of being with my family and friends.

Felt amazing, actually.

"You said you'd help me sort through everything." I glanced sideways at the young woman standing close by, her face unhappy despite our surroundings, the tall man with her hunching his shoulders inside his jacket. Neither of them seemed to have embraced the Christmas spirit.

"I told you," the man said, "just throw it all away. It's been over a long time, Tracey. You need to let this go."

It was clear that wasn't the answer she wanted to hear from him, the rebellion on her face pinking her cheeks past the chill of the air, jaw set, full lips a thin line and, despite her tiny self up against a much taller and bigger man, she seemed ready for a fight, trembling inside her puffy blue jacket and knitted hat.

"I knew this was a mistake," she snapped. "Thanks for nothing, Uncle Kenny." And spun before he could stop her—which he tried to do, to his credit, one big hand reaching for her too late— and marched off through the crowd, pushing people out of her way aggressively. The man she called uncle sighed and turned his back, slouching off in the opposite direction.

I meeped a little when someone hooked their arm in mine, Daisy joining me, face sad.

"How tragic," she said. "It's Christmas. Family is so important this time of year."

Was she talking about the fight between the girl

and her uncle or her own sad circumstances? It was no secret Daisy's absentee father was a piece of work, nor that with her mother's passing, she was rather alone in the world. I hugged her then, refusing that bit of so-called logic. Because while I might have walked away from her, too, when I left, she welcomed me back with open arms and, forevermore, Daisy Bruce would not just be my best friend, but my sister.

Day helped me with the hot chocolate, both of us turning back toward Mom and Dad, practically running headlong into the ivory-clad iron fist who ruled our little town. Olivia looked out of breath and rather peaked, but she paused in her headlong march to the hot chocolate stand to say hello.

"Hope you're enjoying tonight so far," she said in about the darkest and least welcoming tone I'd ever heard.

"It's great," I said, weak smile seeming to mollify her. "Everything looks fantastic."

"It's so beautiful, Olivia." Leave it to Day to gush in her genuine and authentic way that put everyone I knew at ease. Including, apparently, our frazzled and strung-out mayor who flashed my best friend a smile that was more grimace than joy, but it landed anyway.

If the mayor was going to say something to add to that expression, however, she didn't get the chance. Because, before she could speak, a lean, angry woman in a ski jacket with her dark hair tucked under a fur hat—complete with ear flaps—stopped next to us, glaring at Olivia like she'd offended her somehow.

"Where's my money?" Like the mayor was a prostitute and this chick her pimp. She didn't quite hold her hand out for the cash, but she might as well have, while Olivia's expression flattened out and her jaw clenched in response.

"The invoice is with finance," the mayor said. "As I told you earlier, Marion."

"You ordered that tree three weeks ago," the woman Olivia identified as Marion snapped. "Payment was due December 1st."

"If there was a mix-up in the payment, I apologize," Olivia said, though she really sounded like she hated having to do so. "Please stop by the office tomorrow," no stress on that word or anything, "and I'll see to it personally."

"No need." The tall man from earlier appeared out of nowhere, tugging on the woman's arm. "It's fine, Olivia," Kenny said, nodding to Daisy and myself, clearly embarrassed by his companion's attitude. "I'm sure it was just an honest mistake. Right, Marion?"

Marion snorted like there was no such thing when it came to the mayor while Olivia pointedly ignored her and nodded graciously to Kenny.

"Mr. Beckett," she said. "So nice to see you in town for the holidays."

He cleared his throat. "Just here to sort out some family business."

Olivia didn't seem to register that. "I assure you, and Ms. Jackson, the account will be cleared tomorrow. Now, if you'll all excuse me, I have a parade to start." Olivia spun and marched off.

I have no idea what possessed me but seeing her leave without the very thing she'd come for made my heart ache. I chased her, grabbing her elbow. She turned back to me, expression tight until I pressed one of the cups of hot chocolate into her gloved hand.

"You're doing an amazing job," I said, keeping my voice low. Olivia and I didn't always see eye-to-eye, but it was clear she was struggling and doing her best for our town. Someone needed to appreciate her, even just a little. "Thanks for this, Olivia. I'm really looking forward to it."

Her eyes widened just a little and for a moment I wondered if she would speak. Even cry, if the moisture gathering there was warning of impending tears. Instead, she squeezed my now empty hand with her free one before leaving me there to finish what she started while my heart grew a few sizes.

Ah, the Christmas spirit. I really needed to find a way to carry it with me all year.

CHAPTER THREE

When I rejoined Daisy, she was beaming at me, already in line for another cup to replace the one I'd given to Olivia. She didn't comment, but she didn't have to, that sweet expression of hers speaking volumes for her while I felt myself blushing over the simple act of kindness that now had me a bit uncomfortable.

All the more so when I noticed Robert smirking in my direction. If he caught my act and was judging it? He could suck it. Being a nice person who thought of others *would* trigger his sense of bully, the jerk.

Which cut the rest of my odd disquiet over feeling weird about what I'd done out from under itself and restored my happiness.

Arm in arm with Day, I returned to my parents

and, after handing over a cup of steaming cocoa to my Dad, took back the leash to my chubby pug and, with a heave and a grunt, lifted her into my arms, my own hot chocolate at my feet, so the dear girl could see better.

I really was becoming a softy.

The opening song the band played announced the beginning of the parade, though I knew "parade" was a rather generous term for what was about to unfold. Since the entirety of the offering was visible in the square in front of town hall, all the excitement and preparations for the big event were likely to take all of ten minutes—and that included the lighting of the tree behind those ridiculous (and had to be expensive) red curtains.

Instead of my typical cynical eye rolling for the affair, however, I found myself cheering along with the crowd of Reading residents and visitors alike as the marching band started the show, their truly painful renditions of Christmas carols only making me all the happier. Since I'd once lugged a snare drum in one of those exact white and blue uniforms up Main Street and to all the football games we always lost, nostalgia was a welcome friend at the memory of doing my uncoordinated best to use my sticks and walk to the beat without tripping and falling on my face.

Good times.

The band paused at least two minutes, running through several different carols all strung together (I think I recognized "O Holy Night" and "We Three

Kings" before "Little Drummer Boy" marched them on). When they finally started moving again, they didn't go far, splitting up at the top of the corner, forming a wall of music as the cheerleader club took the street, bouncing and leaping and throwing one another in acrobatic moves that actually had me gasping at their skill. And the fact the poor girls in their skimpy costumes had to be freezing as I shivered inside my heavy coat. They didn't seem to care, smiles wide, and not a mistake made before they, too, gave way to the happy and cheerful selection of locals dressed as elves, jingling their way through the crowd, handing out candy canes and tweaking noses.

But no one paid attention after the fanfare began, everyone stopping to watch, my own heart pounding, my face aching from smiling, as the red-painted sleigh came into view from behind yet another red curtain, pulled by horses with reindeer antlers on their harnesses, the driver slouched over, a cigar hanging from his lips, elf costume rather rumpled and exceedingly hilarious, considering. Because, despite his disgruntled appearance, it was the gorgeous couple in the sleigh itself that had everyone screaming in delight, calling out and waving rather excitedly, as our very own Mr. and Mrs. Claus—Dr. Lloyd Aberstock and his lovely wife, Bernice—threw more candy canes into the crowd, their stunning suits, I knew for a fact, custom made just for them.

There was a reason they had that particular job to fill. I'd always thought Dr. Aberstock looked like the jolly old soul himself, and his lovely and adorable wife, Bernice, was so much his perfect partner in the North Pole gig it was impossible to think St. Nick and his bride could look like anyone else.

"Ladies and gentlemen," Dr. Aberstock boomed over the crowd, "hes, shes and theys," I beamed at his inclusiveness, "and my very darling boys and girls," the kids lost their minds. "Christmas is at hand. Join Mrs. Claus and myself, won't you, for the lighting of our tree. Let's welcome the holidays together!"

The sleigh started up again, horses clip-clopping their way to the corner before doing a slow turn to follow the band, cheer team and elves back the way they'd come to town hall. As I waited for the crowd to thin, I set Petunia back on her feet, noticing as I did the young woman from the earlier argument at the hot chocolate cart was standing next to me. She didn't seem to notice I was there, staring into the crowd like she was all alone in the world and, with that same Christmas spirit that had me stop Olivia (and a healthy dose of busybody thrown in for good measure, because I knew myself better than that), I smiled and spoke up.

"I don't think I've seen you in town," I said. She jerked a little, surprised to be addressed, perhaps. But she didn't frown or move away so I stuck out my mitten. "Fiona Fleming. I own Petunia's, the B&B."

She blinked at me, her brown eyes distant, before she finally smiled a little, shook my hand rather perfunctorily. "Tracey Beckett," she said. "Sorry, I'm not really in the mood for this." She stuck both hands in her pockets, looking away again. "I don't even know why I came."

"I used to feel that way," I said. "Took a while, but I finally figured it out."

She grunted softly, shrugged inside her puffy ski coat. "I don't even live here anymore," she said. "Just here to sort out some... family business." Her lips twisted, unhappiness apparent. Funny how she said the exact same thing her uncle did.

I wanted to ask more, but before I could, an older woman in a long winter trench, her narrow head stuffed into a plaid hunting cap and big, heavy boots clomping on the pavement, stopped next to Tracey, glaring at the girl while the younger backed off a half step at the intrusion.

"What do you want, Olga?" Tracey seemed intimidated but angry at the same time.

The older woman's lined face screwed into a grimace before she repeated Robert's act and spit on the pavement, though her offering wasn't quite so impressive.

"You go back to the city," she growled at Tracey. "If you know what's good for you." Shifted her beady, dark eyes to me, overgrown eyebrows wriggling as her deeply wrinkled mouth turned down into a crevasse of unhappiness. "What are you looking at?"

I didn't comment, to which she snorted and then marched on, brushing past Tracey hard enough she clipped her shoulder before carrying on. Then again, as I watched in growing annoyance, the woman Tracey called Olga didn't seem to pick favorites, practically mowing over a pair of little kids before their mother jerked them out of harm's way and kicking the tire of the hot chocolate cart with one boot hard enough to make it wobble.

"Pleasant woman," I said.

Tracey glared after her then shrugged again, the favorite gesture of the twentysomething set. "Olga Nowak is a nutcase," she said, as if that explained everything. "I used to live next door. My dad's..." she paused. "But she's right. I should never have come back here."

"Please, gather round!" That was Olivia on a loudspeaker, microphone in her hand, standing on the little stage next to the red curtains hiding the tree. The sleigh had stopped near the stairs to the platform and Dr. Aberstock had already joined her, helping Bernice with a hand up. When I glanced back to Tracey she'd already gone, though where I couldn't say. None of my business, but Daisy was right. Christmas was no time to be sad and alone.

Leading the happy Petunia toward the tree, I joined my bestie and my parents near the far side of the curtains, close enough I could touch the heavy vinyl if I wanted to. Dad might not have been sheriff anymore, but he knew how to work a crowd. While I was positive a more distant view would give the full picture, the idea of standing right next to the tree as it was lit made my little girl's heart go pitter-pat. With a wicked grin, I ducked past my dad and winked up at him, Petunia hanging back at Mom's feet.

"My fellow Reading residents," Olivia said, "I am delighted to welcome Christmas to our town!"

Something was supposed to happen then, apparently, though it took some hissing whispers from Olivia to the young man standing next to the ropes who tugged furiously on them several times before the curtains finally dropped to the tittering laughter of the crowd. At that same moment, Dr. Aberstock connected the heavy extension cords that would light the tree in our very high-tech Reading celebration.

I loved my town.

Looked up at the towering spectacle lit with multi-colored bulbs and hung with sparkling ornaments.

Froze. Inhaled sharply. And was on the move without thinking, because one of the decorations was not like the others.

Pretty sure Olivia's orders to hang things on the tree didn't include a body.

CHAPTER FOUR

There was something incredibly creepy about a sweet-faced man in a Santa suit crouched over a dead body that would have ruined Christmas for me if said suit wasn't worn by one of my also favorite people, Dr. Aberstock. He, for his part, seemed unphased by the fact he still wore his furry hat and fluffy coat, that his gleaming buttons reflected back the oddly mummified face of the dead man lying on the ground under the glowing Christmas tree.

Someone had failed to turn the lights out even after Crew quickly and efficiently cleared the scene, having Jill and the grumpily compliant Robert herd parade-goers and cheer squad members and crying bandmates out of the square so an investigation could begin. Mind you, said gathering stopped dead (no pun intended) at the corner and, *en masse*, chatted and pointed and made comments about the fact there had been, only a moment ago, a dead guy swinging from the town tree like our very own angel.

Of death, however. Which wasn't really in keeping with the holiday, so whoever put him there? Had a very sick sense of humor. Or something to prove.

"He's not fresh, that's for certain." Dr. Aberstock leaned back on his haunches, wrists resting on his knees. I had trouble balancing that way myself, let alone with a rather portly tummy in the way. The doc never ceased to amaze me. "I'd estimate he was embalmed maybe a decade ago?" He looked up at Crew who had, as yet, to chase me or my dad, the two of us lurking (hey, I called it what it was, because *lurking*) where we'd both come to a halt under the place the body had hung. Either it was Dad's presence that kept the sheriff from giving us the boot or the fact my father helped lower the corpse or even, maybe Crew had grown tired of telling me to mind my own business while not saying so in as many words to Dad but meaning them.

Whatever his reason(s), our sheriff took note of the doc's findings before looking up and meeting Dad's eyes, the inappropriate flashing of my father's antlers remaining unmentioned. The fact Crew pointedly ignored me could have been on purpose, a nod to my being there. Or could have been his unwillingness to deal with me just yet. So many options hovering around, so little time.

"Would have been on your watch, John." That could have come out like an accusation, but Dad took it as Crew meant it while I bristled a little. What was he implying?

Nothing, Fee. He wasn't implying anything. Just stating fact.

Dad, for his part, frowned and nodded. "This is Brian Beckett," he said. "Used to own the Christmas tree farm. I think his brother took it over, Kenny?" I twitched at that, couldn't help it. Wait, the same Uncle Kenny who I'd seen and then met earlier? Tied to that nasty piece of work, Marion, who'd made Olivia uncomfortable and the nice girl, Tracey, I'd just met?

Their mention of family business now had my head spinning.

Crew seemed to notice my reaction because he finally met my eyes, his own guarded, the deep blue catching the flashing lights of the tree and Dad's antlers and reflecting the glow back to me. "You have something?" How careful, that tone, words clipped but not enough for me to call him out on rudeness.

"His daughter and brother are both here," I said. Okay, blurted. "And his neighbor." Don't forget Olga, the creepy old lady. "And someone named Marion Jackson who works at the farm."

See, I didn't set out to upset him, did I? He asked, didn't he? Came out and asked and it wasn't my fault I encountered all of the above said people tonight. If anything, one would think he'd be appreciative of my presence, of the fact I had information to share.

One would think.

Except, we had a history of butting heads and it appeared that wasn't about to change anytime soon, Christmas being the reason for the season or not.

I did give him credit for not losing his crap and storming off, though the jaw jump and the tic had started, so I knew he was already at a slow sizzle. As long as the forehead vein held off, we might be okay. I also considered it a miracle I didn't mutter, "You asked," and for falling silent after delivering the above which, to my amazement, was harder than I thought it would be.

I'm nosy, okay? Get over it.

Olivia's sudden appearance cut off any chance Crew might have had to respond to me, if he even intended to. She huffed so loudly, her face furious and entire being trembling, I decided keeping quiet was probably for the best anyway.

"This is a disaster." She hissed that at no one in particular before spinning on Crew and planting an index finger firmly in his chest, staring up at him like he'd dug up the man on the ground and hung him on the tree personally just to make her life miserable. "I want this taken care of immediately, Sheriff Turner, and I mean *immediately*." She wiped at her mouth with one glove, red lipstick coming off on the ivory wool. It was a testament to Olivia's upset she didn't seem to notice, though I flinched a little at the visual, as though she herself had suffered a fatal blow, and was about to fall before us, another Christmas tree victim.

Hush, imagination. I had more than enough complications in my life at present I didn't need fake ones too.

Instead of dropping like my mind whispered would be just my freaking luck, she spun and marched toward the crowd again, leaving the rest of us to stare after her a moment.

Her attention hadn't eased Crew's own mood, however, so when he fixed that blue-eyed gaze on me one more time, I knew his fuse had finally burned down to the caldera inside him and one false anything would have me kicked out of the scene.

Well, maybe I didn't want any part in his little body problem. So there.

"You said Kenny Beckett." I nodded at Crew's question, his pen almost tearing the paper of his notebook he pressed so hard. Wasn't helping Dad noticed, grinned a little before covering his mouth with one big, gloved hand. Crew realized his temper was showing, cleared his throat. Spoke into his shoulder mike. "Jill, Kenny Beckett, please."

It was only a moment later she was gesturing from the edge of the crowd to the tall man I'd met earlier, his lean, lanky form covering ground in long strides. Pale-faced and trembling, he glanced down at the body before averting his eyes.

"Sheriff," Kenny said. "This is horrible. Is that really Brian?"

Crew pointed at the body. "I need you to make a positive ID, Mr. Beckett," he said.

Kenny looked down again, swallowed hard as

though his stomach threatened a second coming, then jerked his gaze away, nodded. "That's my brother," he whispered. "Who would do such a thing?"

"I take it Mr. Beckett was buried here in town?" Crew's usual soft questioning wasn't present, the harshness of his tone seeming to surprise even him, though Kenny didn't seem to notice.

"He was," Kenny said. "Reading United Methodist Cemetery, attached to the church."

Crew made a note. "Can you tell me, how did your brother pass?" There was the kinder, softer sheriff, the one I was used to even when I participated in investigations without his approval. He usually reserved such tension just for me or for those who angered him, never for the victim's families.

"He hung himself," Kenny said, voice now dull and empty. "Nine years ago today, in fact." That made his presence a sign of something more than a prank, then, perhaps? "On the farm."

The same farm where the evergreen above us, still glowing its happy holiday cheer, had come from? There had been a possibility this was a prank, aimed at Olivia or the council. A sick joke, probably a drunken choice made by some yahoos who didn't know better. Except it was pretty clear to me—and hopefully to Crew—that the possibility of such had died its own death. Yeah, no coincidences here. Someone was sending a clear and unhappy message that likely had nothing to do with Reading and everything to do with Brian Beckett's passing.

But who and why?

"Any idea why someone would do this, Mr. Beckett?" Crew was in full-on professional with a solid side of compassion mode again, though it had no impact on the victim's brother.

Kenny, for his part, didn't snap out of his dull and empty state. "I have no idea," he said. "Why anyone would do this to Brian."

"I remember the case," John said then, that equally kind and grave tone almost a perfect match for Crew's. Did they go to the same cop school or something? I knew they hadn't. Which made me wonder if they butted heads because they were so much alike or maybe that was just me and I needed to admit I was the problem. Yeah, I already knew the answer to that. "Doc, there was a temp coroner in the office that week. You and Bernice were on a cruise, I think."

"Yes, John, to Fiji. As usual, you have an excellent memory." Dr. Aberstock stood and hooked his thumbs in his thick, black belt, looking so Santa-like while the emaciated corpse laid out at his feet gave me chills. "You found no evidence of foul play, did you?"

Dad shook his head, frowning down at the dead body. Only then did he seem to realize he still wore the flashing antlers, sliding them from his head and turning them off, all the holiday cheer gone in that one act I hoped wasn't a bad sign of Christmas disaster to come. "I didn't," he said. "I spoke to his daughter, Tracey." He glanced at me. "Right? You said her name is Tracey?" I nodded, stayed silent, while Dad went on. "Poor thing found her father hanging from the rack where they wrapped the trees for transport. Two empty whiskey bottles." Dad shook his head then. "There was no indication it wasn't suicide."

"Of course, it was suicide," Kenny said abruptly. Stopped, stared at my father. "What else could it have been?"

I didn't say murder. I swear I didn't. But I was thinking it, you better believe it. And from the grim expressions of the two lawmen in front of me, they were, too.

"I told you!" The young woman appeared beside me, shoving me out of her way though I took no offense, considering. Held my ground as Tracey Beckett pushed past Crew too and stared down at the body of her long-dead father. Tears poured down her face when she spun on Dad. "I told you he didn't kill himself." I wasn't expecting her to punch him, but she did, both fists hitting Dad in the chest. He didn't flinch, didn't try to stop her, though she only managed one solid hit and a second more feeble one before her uncle reached out and pulled her away from my father.

"The coroner said there was no evidence, that it was murder." Dad paused and I hated the doubt that crossed his face. He was an amazing cop, had served Reading as sheriff for a long time. I trusted and believed in him and so did the rest of our town. To think he'd made a mistake? Crushing, to be honest, though he'd never know it.

We were all human and you know what? I had to accept my dad wasn't a superhero.

"Miss Beckett," Crew said, "did you have something to do with your father's appearance tonight?" He said it softly enough, in that same compassionate voice he'd found for her uncle.

Instead of letting it soothe her, however, Tracey snarled in response to his tone. "You're disgusting," she said. Sobbed twice, barely breathing, before collapsing to the ground where she wailed her heartbreak.

I went to her immediately, her uncle seeming at a loss, Crew's face tight with whatever he was fighting off at her response. He'd had to ask, I knew it, he knew it, we all did. But the way Tracey crumbled? If she had anything to do with this, I'd eat the damned tree in front of me and call it Christmas dinner.

"John." Crew cleared his throat again, tucking his pen and notebook away, looking up at the tree, squinting into the glow. "I'm going to have to reopen the case."

"Of course, you are," Dad said immediately. "And I'm coming back to the office with you to show you what I have. If this wasn't suicide, if I missed something, I'll make it right." He met my eyes where I hugged the still weeping Tracey. "I promise, Miss Beckett. I'll make it right for you."

Tracey ignored him, jerking free of me, staggering to her feet while Dr. Aberstock spoke.

"It's my honor to review the autopsy," he said. "If something was missed on my counterpart's end, I'll find it."

The EMTs had arrived, making their way through the crowd, heading for our little huddle. I stood, staying close to Tracey, hanging back with her as Crew and Dad left for the sheriff's office, Dr. Aberstock leaving for his car to follow the ambulance, Jill and Robert finally dispersing the crowd while Kenny hovered, looking like he wanted to say something to his niece but not knowing what. Finally turning and walking away in that same hunched and defeated way while Tracey stared at the tree with tears rolling down her face and I took a chance, like I always did, and poked my nose in where it wasn't wanted.

CHAPTER FIVE

"I'm so sorry about your father." I didn't try to touch her again, but felt her sway next to me, looking down at the pavement where Brian Beckett's body had lain only a moment ago.

"No one believed me back then," she said, bitterness and fury mingling with grief as she vibrated with it, so much emotion aging her past her biology. "I was only fourteen. Just a kid. I told the sheriff Dad didn't kill himself. He wouldn't." She spit out that last word with venom. "My father was a jerk, a real ass. No one really liked him, not my mom, not Uncle Kenny. But he was my dad." She sniffled, wiping at her running nose and wet cheeks with the cuff of her jacket. Turned to stare at me with the hurt, lost expression of a little girl who the world let down in the worst way possible. "Promise me you won't let them stop until they find out what happened to my dad."

She didn't have to ask. I'd already made myself that assertion. "I swear," I said. "Tracey, John Fleming is *my* dad." She flinched at that, glanced the way Crew and my father had gone. "He's a good cop. And he meant what he said. If something was missed, he'll find it. He and Sheriff Turner." Not to mention Dr. Aberstock. And yours truly.

I didn't expect Daisy to join us, though I was happy to see her. She held out her hands to Tracey who glanced at me as if unsure of my bestie's intentions before I half-smiled in sorrow and encouragement.

"Daisy Bruce," I said, "Tracey Beckett. It was her father."

Day let out a soft cry of compassion and hugged Tracey. The shock on the girl's face almost made me laugh, if the clear lack of anything resembling familiarity with being comforted hadn't made the whole moment even more tragic.

"Don't worry, Tracey," Daisy said. "Whoever did this, Fee will figure it out. Won't you, Fee?" I opened my mouth to caution my best friend not to go on but she barreled in, didn't she? Both feet and guns of support blazing. "She's solved four murders so far," well, six if you counted the young man haunting Sadie's house and the professor, but who was counting, "and I'm sure she'll be able to find out what happened."

Tracey spun on me then, eyes huge. "You meant it," she said. "You really meant it."

Crew would be pissed, but I nodded. "Every word."

She seemed mollified, wiped at the last of her tears. Sagged against Daisy when my bestie went in for an arm around the girl's shoulders. Mom's appearance, Petunia in tow, seemed to have an even lighter influence on Tracey. She knelt and hugged the pug who licked her wet cheeks happily before groaning a deeply satisfied sound when the girl rubbed her ears.

"It's been quite an evening," Mom said, meeting my eyes with concern there, but keeping her tone even. "Why don't we all head back to Petunia's for a cup of tea?" She smiled sadly down at Tracey who looked up, startled. "You too, Tracey. I think it would do you a world of good. And if my husband and daughter are going to solve this case, find out what happened to your father," Mom had clearly been eavesdropping, and now you know where I got it from, "Fee is going to need all the information you can give her." Tracey looked down at Petunia who meow-yawned at her before panting her sweetness in the girl's face. "Do you think you're up to it?"

Tracey stood, nodded slowly. "Thank you," she said. "For believing me."

If she'd said another word, one more broken and aching syllable, I would have burst into tears myself. Instead, Daisy's arm linked through hers and leading the way, I fell in step with Mom and Petunia and headed home, the evening not quite the happy holiday celebration I'd hoped for.

The cheery decorations at Petunia's seemed slightly less so as we entered the foyer, though I forced myself to shake off the looming doom that had followed us home from town square. Besides, this wasn't about me, the tiny young woman under the big ski jacket looking in need of a solid meal or ten as I relieved her of her coat and stored it in the front closet before following Mom, Daisy and Tracey into the big, bright kitchen, Petunia huffing along in search of treats.

I settled the young woman on a cushion with a bowl of cut-up strawberries and left her to feed the wriggling porkchop who loved every second of their interaction, eyes bulging while Petunia awaited each morsel, corkscrew of a cinnamon bun tail wagging energetically, Tracey's heavy melancholy lifted briefly while she giggled over the pug's antics. When she was done and my fawn creature had licked the bowl clean to her dissatisfaction (that there wasn't more), Tracey joined us at the kitchen island, perching on a stool and leaning into the counter, accepting the tea Mom offered. She'd definitely improved in her mood, even smiling shyly at my mother, at Daisy who patted her hand before Tracey cupped the mug in her tiny fingers and blew on the steam.

"I remember you, dear," Mom said, setting a plate of scotch cookies on the counter, perfectly piped in stars and trees and snowmen, glazed icing artistically applied to the point I always felt guilty biting into them and ruining what Mom made.

Tracey helped herself to one, nibbling a corner. "You do?" She seemed surprised by that. "I wasn't the kind of student you'd remember, Mrs. Fleming."

Mom made a tsking sound. "You loved art to the point Mr. James asked me to give you a free class last semester before graduation so you could focus on applying to art schools." Tracey's face lit up a little. "I was so sorry to hear you moved to Montpelier. I never got to find out if you were accepted, though I'm sure you were."

Tracey nodded then, sipped her tea, much more at ease. "I was," she said. "Went for a year. But Mom got sick, so I had to drop out." She shifted in her seat. "Cancer. Was a long battle." She sighed. "seven years of it. Mom died a week ago." Another fidget, as though she couldn't get comfortable. "That's why I'm here. She had a storage locker, left a bunch of stuff behind she was too sick to deal with when we moved. I'm here to clean it out finally. Move on." Tracey sniffed, wiped at her nose with her cuff even as Mom passed her a tissue. "Nothing was the same after Mom and Dad split. I was eight." She loved to shrug as though such truths would simply roll off her back. "I thought maybe when he married Marion everything would settle down. But they only lasted five years." A deep sigh seemed to deflate her, pale face drawn with worry and weariness and enough grief for a lifetime lived in barely two decades. "Now, maybe, I can figure out what I want to do. But I have to clean up this mess first." Jaw tight again, she pushed her mug away. "Thanks for the tea."

It felt like she was going to bolt, but I had to keep her here if I was going to fulfill my promise.

"You found your father." Yes, it was callous, but a slap in the face might have been what she required to bring her back to the moment instead of losing her in the past, as her distant stare seemed to have done.

She flinched, met my eyes while Mom sighed. Had I gone too far? But Tracey just nodded.

"In the barn," she said. "Where we kept the harvested trees. We'd cut them down then bind them in twine to keep the branches from getting broken." Her hands lifted and seemed to shape something, as though acting out of old memory. "Dad built this machine to do the wrapping because it was really hard to do by hand." Tracey's eyes brimmed, but her voice didn't change, didn't crack or warble. "He drank a lot. Like, a whole lot. I used to find him out in the barn passed out with a bottle in his lap. He never hurt anyone, wasn't that kind of drunk." She used the tissue Mom had handed her on the tears escaping, on her nose, but still maintained that level tone and matter-of-factness that hurt me far more than blubbering would have. How much hurt did one have to endure to create that amount of detachment, to make such a performance possible? I didn't want to know and wish she didn't have to carry it with her. "It was Christmas, and I was helping out. Mom hated it, but it was the only time I had to spend with him, so I'd take December every year and move back to the farm." Tracey hesitated a long moment, took another sip of tea, then spoke. And, when she did, she finally let me hear the pain she bore. "I went outside to check on him. I heard a noise and figured he'd gotten drunk again, was sleeping it off. But when I turned the lights on…" Tracey shook, closing her eyes, unable to speak for a moment while I sat and let her have the time she needed, Mom and Daisy and myself all holding space for her to grieve as, likely, she'd never done before. "He was wrapped up in the rigging, hung." Tracey took the new tissue Mom pressed into her hands but didn't use it yet. "He was already dead, there was nothing I could do. But I still wonder if I'd just gone out to check on him sooner." She shrugged one last time, stared at the tissues in her hands like she had no idea what they were, the jagged edges of her chewed nails showing the remnants of black nail polish chipped to bits.

"There's nothing you could have done," Mom said.

Tracey didn't respond.

"Could he have accidentally been caught up in it, Tracey?" I had to ask that question. She looked up when I did but I didn't stop, needing her to hear me. "It was off when you arrived?" She nodded. "Could the safety switch have turned it off?"

She startled me by barking a laugh. "Um, no offense, but Dad built the thing," she said. "Trust me, there was no such thing as a safety anything on the farm."

"That's why you thought it was murder and not

suicide," I said.

She leaned toward me, lips a thin line of determination. "There's no way he could have gotten in that position on his own, couldn't have reached the switch to shut it down. And I didn't do it. Someone had to have put him on the rack and waited for him to die before turning it off again."

Only one thought crossed my mind and from the way Mom frowned and Daisy went pale they were wondering the same thing as me.

How did Dad miss that?

CHAPTER SIX

Tracey accepted a fresh dose of hot water for her tea when Mom offered up the pot, though she didn't drink much of it as she went on, staring into the steam like it might offer answers she'd never been able to uncover.

"I know you're going to ask me why you think someone would murder Dad." She didn't look up, but the anger on her face told me she was lost deep inside it and had been a long time, didn't need outside affirmation to let it show or build. "Like I said, he wasn't the nicest guy. Actually, he really was horrible to a lot of people." So clear-cut, and without judgment. "But he loved me and was always good to me, even when he was drunk." Dads. I got it. Glanced at Daisy who seemed enraptured by

Tracey's unfolding story, my bestie's eyes shining with unshed tears of her own. So much empathy in one lovely package. Made me wonder why she'd never gone into psychology, though if Day ended up a therapist, she'd be the one in need of drugs because she'd absorb every patient's pain as her own in an attempt to fix them.

"My ex-stepmom," Tracey said then, fingers tightening around the mug so much her knuckles whitened, and she finally did meet my eyes again. Hers flashed fresher anger than what had held her just a moment before. "The divorce was messy, super messy. Went on for months, fighting back and forth. But Dad held his ground and she only got what was promised in their prenup. Bad enough she had shares in the farm." She sat back now, ignoring the cup of tea, the cookies, running her hands over her brown hair, shaking out her ponytail that hung over the shoulder of her knit sweater and clung with static to the pale blue fibers. "She threatened him all the time, even before they divorced." Tracey paused, a flicker of guilt passing over her face. "Thing was, he threatened her back." Sounded like true love. "I don't know if it was enough for Marion to want to kill him, but they got into it pretty bad sometimes. And when Dad died, just before the divorce was finalized? She talked Uncle Kenny into letting her manage the farm. So even though Dad wanted her out, Marion's still there, has been ever since." No bitterness about it, though, nope. Just a heaping pile of steaming resentment that made Tracey's cheeks pink. "And then there's Olga," she rushed on. "That crazy old bat, she was always sneaking onto the farm, snooping around. She and Dad fought all the time. She even has a shotgun she carries with her everywhere." I hadn't seen it tonight, though Vermont did have an open carry law. "I remember him saying one time if he caught her on our land again, he'd shoot her." Tracey's entire being flinched. "He didn't mean it, not really. But maybe something happened, and she decided it was him or her."

I nodded so she'd know I wasn't judging—well, not much—and gestured for her to go on.

"That's pretty much it," she sighed, sagging inside her bulky sweater, tiny hands folded on the counter in front of her, thumbnail picking at the remains of her black polish. "Dad didn't deserve to be dug up like that, no matter what anyone thought of him."

"Of course, he didn't," Daisy said, reaching forward to squeeze Tracey's hand before letting her go again. "We're so sorry."

Tracey seemed surprised all over again. "You're all so kind," she said, hugging herself. "Thanks."

"So, Marion owns part of the farm and manages it?" How did that happen? Shouldn't Tracey end up with her own stake in it? Or had her father cut her out of the will?

Tracey's face twisted again, this time in disdain and accusation. "That's right," she said. "When Dad died, Mom assumed I'd get a stake in the farm. Dad always said I would. Except, it turns out the will gave Uncle Kenny and Marion equal stakes in the

operation. And they decided to team up against me."
Wow, what a family. "They stole the farm out from
under me, forced me to sell my shares. For pennies."
Tracey hunched tighter like she was defending herself
against an enemy we couldn't see. I wondered how
she could have survived so long with so much vitriol
running circles in her head. "It was supposed to be
my future and now I have nothing."

If Kenny Beckett ended up murdered? Or Marion
Johnston for that matter, I'd be having a serious
conversation with the young woman beside me. But
it was clear she had no motive to kill her father. The
opposite. Though I was sure if she had the option,
she'd raise him just to kill him herself for the position
he'd put her in.

"The farm is more than just history and
connection to your father," Mom said like I'd missed
something.

Tracey nodded then, reached for the mug, sipped.
"Dad wasn't a nice guy, but he was a good
businessman. He had arrangements with the state
government, supplied trees to almost every town in
Vermont, not to mention out-of-state contracts. The
farm is worth millions."

Okay then. That was a giant motive she finally
laid out on the table.

"Tracey," I said, "you know I have to ask you
this, but not because I think you had anything to do
with it. To exclude you."

She didn't react, though clearly knew it had been
coming. "I found him, remember?" The bitterness

was back, retreating when she visibly relaxed at my silence. Maybe she was learning to trust and maybe she was just tired of the whole thing but whatever the reason, when she went on her tone had changed to weary. "I was in my room, had gone to bed early. I was asleep, heard a noise outside from the barn." She shivered. "It must have been the rig running that woke me, but by the time I went out to check, it was quiet again." Tracey's hands started shaking, tea sloshing around a little until she set the mug down with a firm thump. "That's it."

"And the exhumation?" I tried to be gentle, but the question had to be asked.

Tracey smiled, surprising me. "You know what? I wish I'd thought of it. Kind of fitting, finding Dad on one of our trees on the same night he died nine years ago. Whoever did this wants the truth to come out." She wrinkled her nose. "More than I did, I guess." When she sighed this time, it was as though she expelled all the emotion she'd shown us in the last few minutes, leaving behind the shell of a young woman trying to fit the pieces of her life back together. "Now that Mom's gone, I just want to put this all behind me. But if there's a chance we can solve Dad's murder," no question in her mind, he was killed, and I was leaning toward believing her, "I'd have gladly gotten a shovel and done it myself."

CHAPTER SEVEN

I left Tracey in the tender care of my mother and best friend, retreating with my phone to dial the church office. To my surprise, someone answered after the second ring.

"Sorry to call so late," I said to the huffy woman's voice on the other end, clearly unhappy to have to answer at eight in the evening. "I'm looking for whoever manages the cemetery."

"This is she," the woman clipped, her crisp tone firmly cranky. "Gertrude Ennis. How can I help you?"

"Ms. Ennis," I said, "my name is Fiona Fleming."

"I've already spoken to your father," she snapped, "and the current sheriff on the matter. I can assure you, Ms. Fleming, I have no idea what happened, how our cemetery could have been desecrated in this manner." Like she herself had been accused of digging up Brian Beckett and displaying him on the town's tree. Either Crew gave her a going over or she was one of those people who jumped to guilty conclusions no matter what was said to them.

"I'm positive you weren't involved, Ms. Ennis," I said in my most soothing Lucy Fleming tone. It seemed to work, the woman expelling a loud a sigh at the other end of the line.

"I should think not," she said. Paused. "I'm here in my office right now looking at the plot map. I've agreed to meet Sheriff Turner," she said his name like he was now a pariah in her view and deserved nothing less than whatever punishment the Lord almighty delivered for being rude and accusatory toward her, "at 8AM tomorrow morning to investigate the site."

"Thank you, Ms. Ennis," I said. "I'll see you then. Please, try to get some rest. I'm sure this will all be sorted out tomorrow."

"Thank you, Ms. Fleming," she said, tone shifting further from affronted to sympathetic. "I look forward to meeting you."

I hung up the phone, not so sure Crew would have the same reaction when I showed up at the cemetery but determined to do so regardless.

When I returned to the kitchen, it was to Mom and Daisy insisting Tracey stay for the night.

"Fee, the poor dear is in that horrible little place on the edge of town." I knew The Summit Motel, wasn't a fan, either, hated sending overflow guests to stay there when Petunia's was full. As it happened, I did have a room free and instantly agreed to the arrangement.

"I don't want to intrude," Tracey said. "I'm just here a few nights."

Daisy was on her feet, pulling the girl up beside her. "Let's take a drive," she said. "We'll gather your things and get you set up, cozy and safe, here at Petunia's. That way you don't have to worry about a single thing."

I really loved my best friend. Tracey went with her without further argument, though she did pause to squeeze my hand on the way past, looking a bit dazed to be taken care of like this. I let them go, returning to sit next to Mom who handed me, not a tea this time, but a cup of coffee, bless her.

It wasn't much of a surprise Dad joined us a minute later, also accepting a hot java, in the middle of our discussion over the case. My father's typical unreadable and granite-like expression seemed cracked around the edges and, when he hugged me before taking a hearty sip from his cup, I saw the doubt once again surface.

"This isn't your fault, Dad," I said.

"John," Mom said, leaning in to kiss his forehead, "what did you find out?"

Dad exhaled a long and heavy sigh, rubbing at his cheeks with one big hand before leaning into the counter over his coffee. "Just what I remember," he said. "Coroner's report said Brian Beckett was drunk, but that the hanging couldn't have been accidental, that he had to have purposely stepped up onto the rig when it was running. No defensive wounds on the body, history of alcoholism."

"Dad, Tracey said the rig he was hung on didn't have a safety switch." I hated to prod him like this, but he had to know if he'd missed something. "Shouldn't it still have been running when she arrived if it was suicide?"

But my father was no slouch when it came to investigating. His eyes held no deceit or evasion as he nodded. "I thought of that, kid," he said. "But what she didn't tell you—or forgot in her grief or even never knew—is that the breaker to the rig had tripped. Which meant it had to have been on purpose, that Brian getting caught up in it overloaded the circuit and shut the thing down before she made it to the barn."

That was a huge piece of information that changed a lot.

Dad wasn't done. "Without any evidence to the contrary, I had to close the case. With the coroner's report ruling it suicide, I didn't have much choice. I did argue with him, though. Wanted the final report to read accidental. But the young doctor, Montrose, insisted there was no way Brian could have been caught up in the rig without doing so on purpose."

"Did you agree with him?" One last poke at the old bear.

My father took a long drink of coffee before answering. "I examined the rig," he said. "From what

I could tell, Montrose was right. The twine feed was just too high, the platform elevated. The only way Brian Beckett could have been caught up in the wrap to hang himself was to put himself in harm's way on purpose."

I sat back then, crossing my arms over my chest. Even as Dad's phone rang. He answered it immediately, putting it on speaker, setting it in the middle of the triangle the three of us made before speaking.

"Hey, doc," he said. "Fee and Lu are here with me."

"I expected no less," Dr. Aberstock's cheery voice replied. "I assume you've reviewed the case from your end by now, John?"

"I have," Dad said, tone heavy. "What did you find?"

"From what I can tell," the doc said, "your notes were complete. As always, John." Dad didn't respond to that, though I could tell Dr. Aberstock wasn't just blowing smoke but being his eternally genuine self. "As for my counterpart, I'm afraid Dr. Montrose wasn't as thorough as I would have been. I blame youth and inexperience, though from what I hear, he's moved on to other specialties, so I hope he's more rigorous in his focus than he was in this case."

"I take it you found signs leading away from suicide," I said.

"Indeed, Fee, that I did." The sound of papers shuffling, and a few keystrokes preceded his findings. "Whoever embalmed the body was equally inefficient. Fortunately for us, as it means the fluid didn't make it to all the veins. Leaving me sufficient blood for testing. As you are aware, Mr. Beckett was an alcoholic, suffered from early stages of cirrhosis of the liver. There was enough residual trace in the blood I extracted to suggest Mr. Beckett, despite his built-up tolerance, would likely have been unconscious, and that's just from the amount of whiskey he'd drunk." And unable to do as Dad suggested, since being passed out meant there was no way he could have hefted himself up and onto the rig without help. "Even more importantly was the missed substance that he'd ingested as part of his night's imbibing."

"He was poisoned?" Dad perked at that.

"More like knocked out," Dr. Aberstock said. "With enough sleeping pills added to his intake to take out a gorilla."

CHAPTER EIGHT

As I expected, Crew wasn't excited to see me when I joined him and Gertrude Ennis the next morning. To his credit, however, he didn't immediately demand I march my redheaded self back to my car and go home to mind my own business, so I took that as a welcome to join the investigation because that was, apparently, all I needed to reassure my inner busybody she had free rein.

I was a master of making all kinds of excuses given the right circumstances,

"You can see," Gertrude said directly to me after a handshake she obviously hadn't offered to the sheriff if his deep frown and agitation told me anything, "Ms. Fleming," another dig that drove his jaws together hard enough I heard the squeak of his molars grinding together from five feet away, "Mr. Beckett's plot isn't exactly in the center of everything." An understatement, considering the empty grave sat on the very edge of the cemetery, with barely a low fence of chain link between it and the woods on the other side of the plot. "We don't employ cameras in this area, I'm afraid, so finding the culprit will be difficult."

I kicked at the ground with the toe of my boot, noting the surface seemed softer than I expected. "How hard would it have been to dig up the grave, Ms. Ennis?"

She tucked her mittened hands inside her wool coat against the chill of the morning while Crew crouched and stared down into the hole in the ground.

"As you are aware," she said, "it's been unseasonably warm this December. Certainly not cold enough to impede digging."

"May I ask," I went on when the sheriff didn't interrupt or try to stop me, "who embalmed Mr. Beckett?"

Gertrude stiffened instantly, Crew's head snapping up, blue eyes now crinkled around the edges and the vein in his forehead making an appearance.

"I did," she said with so much offense in her tone that I let it go immediately. Not because Crew had straightened and was glowering at me, instant guilt I'd gotten the doc in trouble silencing me where nothing else would. "Now, if you'll excuse me. Ms.

Fleming." She glanced at Crew, nodded, didn't speak again. Instead, she spun and marched off toward the church, leaving me alone with the sheriff.

Not my first choice, at least when he was in this kind of mood.

"What is it about this town," he said, that gravel in his voice even rougher than usual, "that every single person in it seems hell-bent on ensuring even the most sensitive information is common knowledge?"

Now, if I hadn't already been in a rather defensive position, I might have been able to rein in my temper and my tongue. However, knowing me as you do, surely you understand how hard it was for me to restrain myself in that moment. No, *impossible*.

As evidenced by my snippy retort (and I claim snippy without guilt).

"Hardly common knowledge," I said. "Just me and Dad."

That didn't mollify Crew in the least. Probably made things worse. Definitely made things worse. And I really needed to learn to keep my mouth shut.

Only one thing would make this right. I had a single shot at it and, in true Fiona Fleming fashion, gave it my all while knowing things could either bend to my favor or go so badly I'd regret even considering what I did next.

Chose to err on the side of sharing and told Crew everything Tracey told me.

There were times I knew I irritated Sheriff Crew Turner to the point of near apoplexy, that I drove him around the bend and back again and, one day, I might be the cause of an aneurysm if he didn't learn to just let me do me and not get so worked up over it. Thing was, the best part about Crew was his willingness to listen, even when he was angry, to take what I learned and fold it into his own investigation without arguing or pulling the mansplaining card. In fact, despite our differences, he more times than not weighed everything I'd uncovered against what he knew and shifted gears in favor of the truth and justice instead of his own ego, which always raised him in my estimation despite our continuing conflict.

Case in point. When I wrapped up what she'd unfolded the night before, informing him of Tracey's whereabouts to his short nod of thanks, finishing with Dad's addition of the circuit breaker and Dr. Aberstock's findings, Crew stared at the ground a moment, brows furrowed over his remarkable blue eyes, hands in the pockets of his sheriff's jacket, before speaking in a low and careful voice.

"From the looks of the ground the body was just dug up last night." He kicked at the dirt, cascade of it loosely falling into the hole. "There's still enough moisture in it that it couldn't have been earlier, considering the above-freezing temperatures we had overnight." Fog when I'd woken confirmed that, though it had burned off already under the lovely warmth of the morning sun, feeling more like late spring than December. "And, if Ms. Ennis can be believed, the grave was intact when she left at dusk."

Wait, he was sharing information back? I held still

and waited for more. Wasn't disappointed.

"Which gives us a very narrow window of time." He looked up then, at me, no sign of his anger visible though I doubted it was completely gone just yet. He was just a good actor and a good cop.

"Without any kind of video footage, it's going to be hard to identify the culprit." I pointed at the ground. "Though there's at least a few footprints that might help."

He nodded, careful and precise. "I'll have Jill look into it," he said. Drew a deep breath. "Fiona." Paused, exhaled. "Fee." Crew shook his head then, smiled, though without real humor. "As always, your input is... helpful." That was a compliment. I took it. "And, as always, uninvited." Hard to hold that gaze when I knew he was right. Except Tracey kind of invited me, hadn't she? No, wait. She'd only come back to the B&B because we'd asked her to. But she'd needed us, needed to talk. To have someone listen to her and believe her. All sophistry, though, and I knew it. Crew seemed to watch the facts spin out into truth in my head before speaking again, this time kindly. "I'm taking this very seriously," he said. "And carefully. For obvious reasons." Dad. He was talking about Dad, wasn't he? I opened my mouth to respond, to deny the need to tread lightly, but Crew was already speaking again. "Your father was an excellent sheriff and still is a brilliant investigator. I value his work and his ethics. I promise I won't twist this against him. If it hadn't been for the coroner's mistake, I'm positive John would have gotten to the bottom of things." Wait, was Crew worried I'd be mad at him for looking into one of Dad's old cases? Had I misread him? "But I need to have the chance to do that without a giant dog and pony show." Ah, the rub. "You have a tendency toward your father's brilliance but without his... finesse." My lips twisted into a wry smile while Crew grinned at me. "You understand what I'm asking?"

"You're trying to protect Dad's reputation and my bull in a china shop methods make that harder." I wasn't stupid.

"I'm glad we see things the same way." Crew chuckled. "I never thought I'd say that about you and me."

I laughed too, though with sadness behind it. There had been a time I hoped we might connect on a more personal level. And, if it wasn't for my penchant for being nosy and solving murders, maybe that would have been possible. Seeing this side of Crew raised that hope again, despite knowing the chances of ever having a relationship with him that wasn't based in conflict and confrontation were pretty slim.

A girl could dream about such things though, right?

"Thank you for sharing what you know," he said, turning and walking off. Stopping a moment, looking back over one shoulder. "I'd appreciate it if you did uncover anything else if you'd let me know." Crew left me there, staring after him, before forcing myself to turn back to the empty grave and the odd sorrow at the lost opportunity.

When I finally pulled myself together, silly girl, I did one final walk around the plot, pausing near the fence to look out into the woods.

Spotted the footprints and drag marks just inside the tree line.

And, in true busybody fashion, acted before I could think about what Crew just asked of me, hopping the chain link to investigate.

CHAPTER NINE

I could have called Crew, of course, I could have. Wouldn't have been a huge effort to just turn and yell his name, even. He wasn't entirely gone from the parking lot yet when I hopped the fence. I even heard the rumble of his truck engine starting when I ducked into the undergrowth onto the path just a few feet from the edge of the trees.

Thing was, he didn't notice I'd gone, wasn't paying attention, obviously, because despite the fact I half expected him to show up out of the blue because he'd been watching me and noticed I'd already reneged on our so-called bargain (wait, had I agreed to it in a way that could be upheld in a court of law?) I followed the tracks and drag marks alone and on my own, not a sniff of Crew Turner to be found.

The soil was soft on the edge of the path, which led right to a dirt road behind the church. Wait, I knew this road. It led around the property and to the other side of town, one of those local bypass roads tourists never used but those of us from around these parts used as shortcuts when necessary. Mind you, the bumpy and rutted way wasn't exactly photoshoot ready, nor kind to shocks and car undercarriages, enough puddles skimmed with ice thanks to the cool shelter of the trees lowering the temp to just freezing and heaves to make even the most hearty Reading resident wary unless in possession of a 4X4.

I paused at the edge of the road, noting tire treads that looked more rugged than the average car. The footprints ended there, as did the drag marks. So, whoever did the digging up of the corpse had a vehicle waiting to transport the uncovered goods.

Which led to a dead-end (what was with the puns already?). The trouble was the road itself was hard-packed enough the tire indentations vanished the moment they left the softer edge and carried the body away. At least I knew now how and where, which meant the possibility of some kind of trail after all.

I reached for my phone as I hopped the fence yet again and headed for my car. The number I dialed, however, wasn't Crew Turner's.

"Hey, Jill," I said when the deputy answered, my friend's greeting happy enough. "I need to tell you something and I don't want you to get mad."

She laughed on the other end of the line, and I could almost see her tall, broad-shouldered self with her blonde ponytail bouncing under her knitted hat, grinning at her phone.

"Let me guess," she said. "You found something out about the case and if you call Crew he'll be pissed."

"We just had a conversation," I said carefully. "I don't want to disappoint him."

Her chuckle made me grin in return. "Just tell me," she said. "I'll make sure he finds out from me."

I filled her in on what I'd stumbled over while she grunted softly in reply.

"I'm on my way there now," she said. "I'll take a look. Thanks, Fee. Very helpful."

"Happy to hear it," I said. "At least you appreciate me."

She laughed one more time, the sound of her car door closing and engine firing up in the background. "You make me look good," she said. "I'll keep you posted." And hung up.

Okay then.

I was just pulling up to Petunia's when my phone rang, Dr. Aberstock's number flashing. "Hey, doc," I said.

"Fiona," he said in that cheerful tone of his. "I tried to reach your father but he's not answering. Can you pass something along?" Which was code for here's some information Crew likely wouldn't want me to have but Dr. Aberstock, on the other hand, wasn't even hesitating to hand over.

I loved that man. "Sure thing," I said, grinning all over again. "I'll make sure he gets it."

"Just confirming it was sleeping pills," the doc said. "And since Brian Beckett didn't have a prescription for such medication, I'm calling it murder."

"I'll make sure Dad knows," I said. "Thanks for the confirmation."

"Fee." Dr. Aberstock cleared his throat on the other end of the line. "You know I adore your father. John Fleming is one of the best cops I've ever worked with. His record is stellar. This isn't his fault."

I sighed and nodded though he couldn't see me. "I know, Dr. Aberstock," I said. "Mistakes happen to the best of us. But you know Dad's blaming himself."

"I do," the doc said. "Because that's the kind of man your father is. No matter what the circumstances, he holds himself accountable. Please, if you can talk to him, assure him if I'd been in the office the night Brian Beckett was brought in, he'd have had a case to pursue instead of this unhappy revisit. And also assure him," his tone changed to firm and almost angry, "I'll be reviewing each and every case Dr. Montrose oversaw during my vacations, under a microscope."

"I'm sure he'll be relieved to hear it." I thought about it a moment, then asked a question. "Doc, how would I go about finding out who in Brian Beckett's life had a prescription for sleeping pills?"

Dr. Aberstock didn't hesitate. "The investigating officer should be able to look into that, even after the fact," he said. Suggesting loud and clear I talk, not to Crew, but to my father. The fact the doc suggested I bypass the sheriff wasn't lost on me, nor was his then cheery goodbye.

I hung up then, grateful for Dr. Aberstock and his kindness. Knowing it wouldn't matter, not to Dad, but hoping it might at least give my father a modicum of comfort.

Yeah. Because John Fleming was forgiving of himself when he dropped the ball. Time to give him a shot at making things right once and for all.

CHAPTER TEN

If I expected to find Dad in a funk, I was sorely mistaken. In fact, when I arrived at my parent's house (Petunia in tow and the staff left in charge), I found my father at the kitchen peninsula, Mom making coffee and Dad on the phone.

"Thanks, Don," Dad said, hanging up as I stopped to hug him, then circled to hug my mother, accepting the mug of coffee from her while she poured another for Dad.

"Dr. Aberstock called," I said.

Dad nodded, pushing a notepad toward me, his heavy handwriting legible for once. "Already had a chat with Lloyd," he said. "That was Don Pierce, at the pharmacy. Looks like we have two suspects to chat with."

"They both had scripts for sleeping pills?" I arched an eyebrow at the list. That meant Tracey's suspicions about her uncle were correct, Kenny Beckett having been prescribed the pills. So, it turned out, had her mother, Jayne. With Tracey's mother dead, was there even a way to find out if she was a viable suspect?

And, if she had killed Tracey's father, would it serve anyone to deliver that news to her still grieving and now orphaned daughter?

"You're thinking what I'm thinking," Dad said, grimacing and shaking his head.

"Surely you don't think Jayne had anything to do with it?" Mom seemed shocked by the suggestion.

"We can't rule her out yet, Mom," I said. "We only have Tracey's story to go by at this point. And, if truth be told, while I believe her, this means she had access to the murder weapon herself. Since she found the body…"

Dad didn't comment on that. "The timing is rather telling."

I sighed, hating this line of thought but knowing better than to let it go. "Considering Jayne just passed, Tracey and Kenny are back in town at the same time… yeah, Dad. There has to be a connection."

Mom tsked softly, but more out of pity and sorrow. "That poor girl," she said. "She's had a hard life, dear thing. I can't imagine what she's going through."

Dad pushed back from the counter, slapping

both big hands on his thighs. Any outward appearance of guilt over fumbling the case had been smothered in my father's typical confidence. "Then let's either get her the answers she's looking for. Or."

"Put her in prison where she belongs." I set down my own cup. And told him what I found at the cemetery along with what I learned from Gertrude and Crew.

"We need to go back to the scene of the crime," Dad said, heading for the door. I followed, slipping into my coat and boots while Mom hovered, looking worried. When she hugged me, Dad's brief kiss to her cheek preceding his march out the door to his truck, she whispered in my ear. My mother didn't hesitate when I arched an eyebrow at the panting pug sitting on her feet, babysitting the least of her concerns. "I'm worried about him," she said. "He blames himself."

"I know," I whispered back. "We'll figure it out, Mom. That'll help."

She blinked at me, tears brimming, but forced a brave smile and a wave for Dad.

I had amazing parents.

I followed him rather than going with him, wanting my own car. It was a short ride to the farm, the large "Evergreen Acres" sign pointing me in the right direction even if I wasn't on Dad's heels.

The long drive, flanked by Christmas trees in training, ended abruptly in a large, open yard, big, white house wrapped in a veranda across from the entry, far left filled with a huge warehouse, the steel roof shining in the sun. But it was the tall form of Kenny Beckett standing next to the company truck, clearly arguing with the smaller and yet no less fierce Marion that caught my attention.

They didn't seem to notice we'd arrived, were still shouting at one another when Dad and I got out of our respective vehicles and headed their way. Kenny finally realized they had visitors, looked up as Marion said something about a payment, the angry owner now contrite and almost embarrassed, though the woman who managed the farm didn't seem to care if we saw them fighting.

"John Fleming," Kenny said, shaking Dad's hand. "And Fiona, correct?" I nodded, shook as well, though when I turned to offer my hand to Marion she ignored the gesture, hands tucked into her pockets, face grim and cheeks still flushed from the words they'd been having.

The sound of another truck pulling up had me wincing. Impossible not to guess who might be behind the wheel, though when Crew joined us, he didn't seem upset, merely polite when he, too, shook Kenny's hand.

"Mr. Beckett," the sheriff said. "I have a few questions."

"Of course," the farm owner said.

"I understand you take sleeping pills." I almost gaped at Dad's audacity, the blunt way he just blurted that out. Caught the clench of Crew's jaw and, on impulse, reached out and tugged just a fraction on the sheriff's cuff. His gaze slid sideways to me, and I bit my lower lip, hoping he got the message.

Dad needed this.

Wouldn't you know? Crew was smarter than the average bear. Let my father carry on, while Kenny stuttered.

"I used to," Kenny said. "But I've been doing hypnosis for my insomnia the last few years." Frowned finally, as though trying to resume control. "Why is it any business of yours?"

"Because," my father said, "your brother," he nodded to Kenny, "was murdered and it's time the truth came out."

They both gaped at him. Kenny's face crumbled, Marion's eyes filling with tears. Their anger gone, they turned to one another, Kenny hugging his brother's ex-wife who cried on his shoulder a moment before they pulled free and got themselves together.

Quite the act if Tracey was to be believed. "I'd heard your divorce was less than amicable," I said before I could stop myself.

Marion jerked like I'd slapped her. "We might not have survived our marriage, but I still spent years with the man," she said. "I loved him once. To find out he didn't kill himself, that he was murdered…" Marion looked away, wiped at her eyes.

"Didn't stop the two of you from undercutting Tracey's part of the farm," I said. Well now, there you were, righteous rage for the little guy. I wondered when it would show up.

Kenny looked distinctly uncomfortable, ashamed,

even, but Marion just shrugged.

"That's business," she said. Wow, classy. "How did Brian die?"

I managed to stay quiet, Dad, too, while the sound of a car pulling up, a door opening and closing behind us, distracted me. Leaving it to Crew to fill in the gaps.

"He was drugged," the sheriff said. "Sleeping pills laced in his whiskey. Whoever killed him dosed him first to make sure he wouldn't wake up when they hung him in the rig."

While I wasn't surprised when Crew showed up, I have to admit I wasn't expecting the next person who joined us, though perhaps it shouldn't have been a surprise when Tracey pushed her way past me, almost throwing herself on Kenny.

"You killed him!" She screamed at her uncle before spinning on Marion. "You both did." She threw a photo at her ex-stepmother before collapsing into sobs. "I hate you!"

Dad caught Tracey, supporting her, while I relieved the shaking Marion of the photograph her former stepdaughter used as a weapon against her. Glanced at it, eyebrows rising in surprise, not just at the content (that was revealing enough, as in lacking clothing and decorum between Kenny and Marion) but the date stamped on the corner from the camera that took it.

"Looks like you two were closer than you let on." I handed it to Crew who frowned down at it before looking up to meet Kenny's now guarded gaze.

"You were having an affair," the sheriff said. "And this photo is proof of that." He looked back and forth between the two of them, both becoming more visibly uncomfortable by the minute, Kenny barely able to meet the sheriff's eyes, Marion's face bright red. "Since this image is dated a year before Brian's death and was in the possession of Tracey's mother," Tracey had to have found it in Jayne's storage locker, there was no other explanation for its sudden appearance, "I can only assume at the very least she knew of the affair." Neither of them spoke. "The question is, did she tell Brian?"

Because, like it or not, here was yet another motive for murder.

CHAPTER ELEVEN

"You were here that night." Tracey had pulled herself together sufficiently to throw that at her uncle. Kenny didn't argue as she went on. "That's why I went to bed early. You and Dad were arguing again. And drinking." She pushed my father away, but not roughly, as though she needed to stand on her own two feet. "Did you kill him, Uncle Kenny? Did you murder my father?" She choked on that question, jabbing an index finger at Marion. "For her?" Tracey didn't even look at the woman now staring at her own boots like her guilt wouldn't let her face the girl she'd once called stepdaughter.

Kenny didn't answer, though Crew didn't seem to take that as a reason not to act.

"Mr. Beckett," the sheriff said with grim intensity,

"I think you'd better come to the office and answer a few questions there. Shall we?"

The fact Kenny didn't argue, seemed dazed and almost confused, meant he didn't fight Crew's request and, a few minutes later, the two were driving off in the sheriff's truck.

I was surprised when Marion broke her frozen stance and guilty hover and made a move for Tracey, trying to hug her. "Tracey, honey, I'm so sorry—"

But whatever it was Marion was going to apologize for—cheating on her father, having knowledge of his murder or just plain grief over how things turned out—she didn't get the chance to finish. Tracey spun and ran off, heading for the big warehouse, while Marion covered her face in both hands and started to cry.

I left Dad with the grieving woman and headed after Tracey, finding her, a moment later, just inside the door to the tree storage. The dim light and almost overpowering scent of evergreen made me pause, my eyesight adjusting slowly to the change in illumination. Tracey hadn't turned on any lights so by the time I'd blinked away the bright sunlight she had closed the distance between herself and the large rack in the middle of the room, staring up at it with tears running down her cheeks.

I winced at the sight of the monstrous thing, twine running from large spools on one end, winding through rings down the center of the long machine, a completed tree trussed like a Christmas goose standing on the far end. And, upon examining it and the height at which the twine began, had to agree with my father and the otherwise slacking Dr. Montrose. No way could Brian have accidentally been caught up in it. He had to have been placed there, like one of the very trees he harvested.

"I haven't been back here since Dad died," Tracey whispered. "I thought I could do this, go through Mom's stuff. But it's so hard, Fee." She hugged herself and I hugged her, too. "What am I going to do?"

"You're going to accept more help," I said. "Day and Mom and I will come to the unit with you. We're happy to sort things out." She almost fought me, but I turned her to face me. "You don't have to be alone, Tracey. There are people in the world who really want to be there for you."

"But why?" She almost wailed that. "You don't know me. Why do you care?"

"Mom knows you," I said. "And even if she didn't, it's... just the way we are."

A little snuffling, some dabbing at her face with her sleeve and she nodded. "Thank you," she said, voice cracking. "I've never had anyone I could rely on. Mom was so sick all the time and no one seemed to care."

My heart broke for Tracey and, in that moment, even if she confessed to me she'd killed her own father I would have moved heaven and earth to make sure she got away with it. Because no one should have to feel so alone they didn't know how to accept help.

"Let's go," I said, guiding her to the still-open doorway. "The past lives here, Tracey. But you don't have to anymore."

I had just waved her off, seeing her drive away with the promise she was going back to Petunia's to lie down, when I noticed movement near the corner of the building. Dad had disappeared though his truck remained, so I could only assume he was inside the house talking with Marion. Curious, I headed toward the motion and, on doing so, spotted a startled face that I recognized before the woman spun and disappeared.

Olga Nowak was living up to Tracey's accusations of snooping, apparently. Since I, too, shared that particular moniker, I figured following her was the most logical option, one busybody to another.

Trouble was, she knew the terrain and I didn't, so it wasn't until I was red-faced and panting, wishing I'd worn a lighter coat despite the descending chill now replacing the spring-like warmth of the morning, that I realized I'd come to the edge of the tidy evergreens and into some heavier underbrush.

The only way I knew I'd reached the property line? One, a barbed-wire fence that had a section cut out of it—not the owner's choice, I was sure—and the business end of a double-barrel shotgun pointed at me as Olga turned to level her weapon with threatening intent.

"Take one step past that fence," she said, "and I'll shoot you for trespassing."

I gaped at her audacity. "Considering I just

chased you off someone else's property," I snapped back, "you might want to think that option over."

"Prove it," she snarled.

Oh, she did not just go there. "Listen, crazy lady," because I was in no mood to deal with this right now, thank you very much, "you either put that gun away or I'll make sure you never get a chance to cross onto this property again, let alone your own."

Maybe an empty threat, but she seemed to take it seriously, lowering the weapon, grimacing at me in return. Even as my phone buzzed, a text coming in.

I checked it despite the furious and clearly cracked walnut with the shotgun still staring in my direction like she was looking for a reason to pull the trigger. Was very glad I did, since the text was from Jill and held some very interesting information I felt rather vindictive about considering the circumstances.

Wildlife cam on the road caught the perp, my deputy friend sent. Along with a photo. Of none other than the woman I faced right now, driving an ATV with a trailer on the back, the corpse of Brian Beckett in clear view.

I looked up, met her squinting eyes. Turned my phone toward her. "Looks like the odds of my threat are about as real as yours." She grimaced, the gun barrel rising again. Oddly, I wasn't afraid, more furious than anything. "You do know digging up bodies is a felony?" What in the heck possessed her to exhume her neighbor's corpse nine years later?

"Olga." I hadn't heard Dad approach, saw the

woman flinch, the gun pivot in her hands. But when she saw it was my father, she lowered the weapon again, turning her head as if embarrassed for him to find her like this. "Have you met my daughter, Fiona?"

Olga grunted something that might have been hello but likely wasn't. "I didn't hurt nobody, sheriff," she said. "Minding my own business."

My father didn't correct the use of that title. "You dug up Brian from his grave, Olga," Dad said, slightly amused. She grinned at him suddenly, showing gaps in her teeth. "That's hardly minding your own business." Okay, clearly Dad had history with this whackadoodle, so I let him deal with her. Since my methods had more than likely been leading me down a path that would have ended up with buckshot and blood. "Why did you do it?"

She abruptly repositioned her gun, opening the stock, tucking it under her arm in a practiced move that proved to me she not only knew her way around it but was probably a better shot than my dad. "It's personal," she said.

"You and Brian had a relationship?" Dad seemed surprised by that.

But when Olga snort-smiled and he-hawed a braying laugh, it was clear he'd missed the point.

"I want access to the land," she said, eyes bright. "He said I could use it. I used it all along." Tracey said she'd been trespassing. That Brian fought with her over it. But I didn't call her on that, let her continue. "And then he died and that moron," she snarled, shifting back to furious and mad, "and the woman he was banging," so she knew about the affair, "went and ruined everything."

"What's on the land you want, Olga?" Dad's gentleness shouldn't have surprised me, his easy nature with the old woman.

Worked, too, how she went all soft and sweet on him. "You won't tell nobody?" Dad shook his head while she glanced side to side like someone might overhear before whispering loudly enough I was sure they heard back on the farm, "Mushrooms."

Dad's eyebrows shot up while I choked on a laugh. "The magical kind, Olga?" He tsked at her but she shook her head.

"The expensive kind," she retorted, digging something out of her pocket, showing us a small, thin strip of white and dark. "The kind chefs in New York pay hundreds of dollars for. Each."

Holy heck.

Even Dad was floored by that. "They grow here?"

"On my land," she sounded proud of that. "And over there." She grunted then, pointing over the fence. "Brian let me pick his, kept the oaks and beeches intact. That's what's needed, oaks and beeches and a certain kind of soil and mountain air." She scowled into the woods toward the main house. "Then Brian died and his brother and his little whore started cutting them all down and putting in those ridiculous evergreens." She spat on the ground. "No more mushrooms." She pointed to the right.

"They're planning to dig up the last grove in the spring. I had to do something."

"Olga, do you know something about Brian's death?" Dad sounded sad. "You could have told me then, you know. When I asked you."

She shrugged, though she did seem ashamed. "Didn't hurt me none," she said. "Just kept picking. Except it's hurt me lots since and it needs to stop." She grit what remained of her teeth. "If he goes to jail, will they leave the trees alone?"

Dad inhaled very slowly before answering. "Olga," he said, "do you have evidence that Kenny killed Brian?"

She blew a raspberry into the chill air. "Saw them go in the barn that night," she said. "Kenny came out. But Brian never did."

CHAPTER TWELVE

I sat on a plastic container filled with kitchen contents (according to the masking tape strip on the top) and sorted through the file folder Tracey handed me, Daisy perched nearby going through a box of assorted items. Mom hadn't been able to join us, still home with Petunia in her possession, but promised to come later that afternoon, not that it mattered. Having us there seemed to have lightened Tracey's spirits somewhat. She didn't seem surprised or all that upset when I told her what I knew, though hearing from me that it was more than likely her uncle killed her father that night should maybe have been more impactful.

Except, of course, she'd already reached that conclusion on her own.

"You're sure he did it?" Tracey's tone wasn't empty enough for me to worry she was stuffing her emotions down, just sad and curious.

"Crew seems convinced," I said. "And Dad. There's a lot of evidence."

"Yes, but are you convinced?" Tracey seemed intent on that question, so I rolled it over before replying.

"I don't know," I finally said with a sigh. "I wish it was cut and dried for you, Tracey. But sometimes the best we get is mostly sure."

She nodded at that, went back to her own sorting.

Daisy had thought to bring her music and portable speaker so we had Christmas tunes to listen to while we worked. I smiled as Daisy called Tracey over and the two leafed through a photo album, the young woman pointing things out to my best friend as they went. And I realized this wasn't actually about going through Jayne's stuff to get rid of it, but a chance for Tracey to reconcile herself with her past and move on.

Something I was enthusiastically in agreement with.

I flipped through the folders, came to one marked with Brian's name, opened it while the strains of "Hark the Herald Angels Sing" melded with Daisy and Tracey's giggles, and felt the entire world come to a heaving stop. Forced myself to breathe while I read the contents. Glanced at my bestie, knowing shock had to be the only expression registering on my face, caught her surprise and quick nod.

Message received. I had something I needed to look into, and I didn't want Tracey involved until I knew the truth of it.

"Sorry," I said, standing quickly after tucking the file into my coat, "I have to run to Petunia's for a minute."

"It's okay," Tracey said, Daisy waving me off. "Thanks, Fee. For everything."

I fired up my car in the gathering dusk come early this far in December, hoping to add to that gratitude of hers. Because if what I'd just read was correct? Cut and dried might be her Christmas present after all.

So, I know what you're thinking. Calling Crew, calling Dad, calling Jill, heck, calling anyone would have been the smart thing to do. Except, I had this weird worry that I was wrong, jumping to conclusions, and, if I was going to be honest, needed to prove it to myself before I dragged anyone else into my guesswork. Because the faster I drove to my destination, the more I doubted I was right and the further along the path of questioning my reasoning I walked until I was climbing out of my car in the yard at the farm.

To the sight of Marion hastily shoving suitcases into the back of her car.

And had my guesses confirmed after all.

She gaped at me a moment as I closed the distance between us, a deer caught in headlights she knew were going to be her end. Everything in her expression, in the fear and darting panic in her eyes, screamed guilty while I fished out the file and showed it to her.

"You had a prenup," I said, Tracey's mention of it brought into evidence physically in the papers I showed her ex-stepmom. "One that stipulated if you cheated on Brian, you'd lose all your shares in case of a divorce."

Marion snarled at me. "Where did you get that?"

"Jayne had it," I said. "Turns out she cared about Brian more than you ever did." Had Tracey's mother ever stopped loving him? No way of knowing now, though she'd certainly done her best to keep an eye on him despite their parting. "Just like she had evidence you broke that agreement with Kenny long before you filed for divorce."

Marion didn't have the right to so much anger, not after what she'd done. "You have no idea what he was like," she said.

"Never got the chance to meet him," I said. "Alive that is. Since you murdered him." I tsked at her. "For money, Marion, really? Shares in the farm? Did Kenny know what you were planning? Did the two of you set this up so you could control the farm and cut Tracey out?" Despicable, horrific.

"Tracey had controlling shares without Kenny's help." Marion's eyes darted left and right. Looking for a way out? I was between her and the driver's seat of her car, so there was no exit that way. Though I had her where I wanted her, what exactly was I going to do with her? Way to think things through, Fleming. "I knew Brian had the photos, said he had proof of the affair. He was going to cut me out, after putting up with him for years." She thought he owed her, huh?

"This farm worth his life, Marion?" Yes, I was baiting her. I needed her off balance, at least long enough to figure out a plan to corner her and take her in. Or talk her into turning herself in. Like my life ever went that easily.

Oh, and by the way, the whole *what was the worst that could happen* question from last night? Regretted it, down to my toes.

She didn't answer that question, rage turning to cunning as she spoke. "I heard him fighting with Kenny that night," she said. "I snuck onto the farm to talk to Brian, to make him see reason. He didn't say anything about the affair. They were fighting about other things, stupid things. Contracts and planting. The usual." She shook then, trembling all over, staring at the suitcases she'd managed to cram into the trunk of her sedan. "I waited until Kenny left, offered Brian a bottle. An olive branch." Marion barked a laugh. "Laced with Kenny's sleeping pills." Of course, she had. She might have had an affair with her husband's brother, but it was clear she held him in about the same esteem as she did the man she murdered. "Didn't take long to knock him out. Though it was an effort to get him on the rig." She wasn't a big woman, and all that dead weight (puns, oy!), I could only imagine. "It did its job when I turned it on. I watched him hang." Zero remorse there. The woman was a monster. "I tripped the breaker on the way out, so it would look like suicide, and slipped out just in time. I almost ran into Tracey." Wait, there was grief, but for the girl. And when Marion met my eyes, hers were wet. "I love that child," she said. "I never wanted to hurt her."

"But you were fine stealing her part of the farm from her," I said.

Marion flinched. "That was Kenny's idea," she said. "I couldn't afford to rock the boat. Not after what I'd done."

Leaving the door open for Tracey to lose her legacy along with her father.

"Why didn't Jayne use the photos against you to trigger the prenup?" If she had cared about Brian…

"She didn't have the prenup," Marion said. Pointed at the file folder. "Those papers were Brian's. She must have had some of his things mistakenly transferred to her when he died. I lost track of them when the house was emptied after his death. I was going to burn them. Didn't get the chance." She shook her head. "Just bad luck."

"And about to get worse," I said. "When you come with me and tell the sheriff the truth."

I saw it in her face the instant she made the choice, but I was still too slow to stop her. Which meant, the moment Marion Jackson leaped into action and ran for the barn, I was swearing my fool head off and racing in pursuit.

This time when I passed through the door into the warehouse, it was so dark I stumbled, and that saved my life. As I fell to one knee, I heard the swish of something passing over my head, caught the reflection of the light from the yard on metal and lunged forward, catching Marion at the knees and sending her falling backward with a shriek. The ax she'd tried to decapitate me with clattered to the concrete floor, her own head hitting hard enough I heard it bounce.

Panting, leaning against the unconscious woman beside me, I pulled out my phone and dialed a familiar number, knowing for once I wasn't going to mind hearing Crew yell at me for not minding my own business.

At least I still had the ability.

CHAPTER THIRTEEN

Petunia trotted through the healthy two inches of snow that had fallen overnight, her little paws stirring up the fluffy fall, her cute little red coat barely fitting her girth despite the fact she was on a continual diet.

The afternoon air carried the scent of the town's tree toward me, the lights already glowing though dusk was just settling around us, the main attraction looming over the square. Snow definitely made things feel more festive, despite the fact Olivia had, dead body adorning it only a few days ago or not, decided to leave things as they were. Which meant, of course, lots of chatter about bad luck and corpses at Christmas that I found oddly amusing despite the gravity of the situation.

It wouldn't have been Reading if there wasn't

drama, after all.

I'd only this morning attended the reinterment of Brian Beckett, Daisy holding Tracey's hand on one side while I did the same on the other, my parents flanking us, even Crew there as the minister said a few words. I'd been a bit surprised Kenny joined the ceremony, though Tracey informed me she and her uncle had a long talk about the past and, in doing so, came to an agreement.

Turned out now that Marion was going to prison for murder, her shares reverted to Kenny. Who, in turn, gave them—without asking for payment—to Tracey, restoring her legacy and, it seemed, giving both of them a new start.

"I guess I'm staying in Reading," Tracey told me in the parking lot after the service, her uncle lurking nearby. She seemed the most content and even happy she had since we'd met. "Since I'm suddenly half owner of the farm and Uncle Kenny lives in Atlanta."

He joined us then, arm around her tentative but not rejected. "It's my biggest regret," he said, "choosing business over family. I finally get a chance to rectify that. We're still working things out," Tracey nodded but smiled, "but I can't think of anyone better to run the farm for both of us."

When I considered that, according to Dad, Olga had her own happy ending, I couldn't help but wonder about the magic of the holidays. Crew agreed not to press charges when Kenny and Tracey insisted, instead pairing up with their neighbor in the mushroom business. Amazing how such solid wins could come out of sorrow.

I had run into Crew on my way to my car outside the cemetery, paused to talk where he leaned against his truck, watching my father shake Kenny's hand.

"All's well that ends well, I suppose," he said. Met my eyes, tense and still unhappy, though his anger had lost its edge since he arrived at the farm to take Marion into custody.

"You're still mad," I said.

He shifted his weight from one foot to the other. "Someone I know has difficulty with boundaries and agreements."

"Someone I know," I said rather archly, "assumes the boundaries and agreements he dictates are actually mutual without confirmation."

Crew grunted then. "You're saying I want to believe you listen to me."

I didn't comment, not even when he sighed and shrugged, turning to open his truck door.

"I'm having a gathering at Petunia's tonight," I said, my mind stumbling over my heart's weird impulse to bring it up. Crew hesitated while I went on, cheeks pinking and brain chastising me for even mentioning it because no way was he going to say yes. "Friends and family. A little Christmas party." Crew's silent staring made me even more nervous. "You're welcome to come, if you want. 6PM." And I'd clearly lost my mind because the last place Crew Turner wanted to be was anywhere near me.

"I'm not family," he said then, voice oddly soft.

Paused, eyes quiet and curious.

"No one should have to be alone at Christmas," I said then, more abrupt and sharp than I meant to be, put off by his attitude, by my own continuing attraction to him despite the fact we would never, ever see eye-to-eye. "Come if you want. The invitation stands." I walked away then, head high, heart pounding and internally berating for putting myself into a position where he could reject me.

Hurt more than it should have, frankly.

I paused by the big tree, smiled up at it, memory of that moment with my burning cheeks as I drove away and refused to look at Crew still giving me the uncomfortable train wreck sensation I seemed to cultivate when it came to the handsome sheriff.

Whatever might come, I was home and whether he liked it or not, I wasn't going anywhere. Or changing a single thing about me.

So there.

We were home in lots of time for a shower, to give Petunia a thorough brushing and tie her cute Christmas bandana around her neck before Mom and Dad arrived, Daisy right behind them. I took a moment to admire the deep emerald dress I'd chosen for the evening, loving the color's complement to my hair color. Not my usual shade, tending toward jeans and flannel or t-shirts, but it was Christmas, so a little extravagance was acceptable, right?

Jill was next to arrive, looking amazing in a dark suit, the Aberstocks caroling their way through the front door, the bells jingling them inside. Daisy had already fired up the music, the appearance of Tracey and Kenny a nice surprise, a few other friends rounding out the seats at the dining room table while Mom whipped up a delicious meal and the festive spirit I'd been longing for filled me to the brim.

I was just passing out the champagne when the door jangled one last time, turning me on the ball of my high heel, smile already in place. Drank in the tall, dark-haired deliciousness who'd decided to join us after all and felt that smile I'd been wearing turn to something a little bit more satisfied.

Left the others to their own recognizance to join Crew at the door, taking his wool trench coat, a dusting of falling snow on his shoulders, in his dark hair, trying not to stare at the rare sight of him in a suit, dark blue shirt the color of his eyes open at the collar two buttons, black curls swept back from his forehead.

He held out a wrapped box, the beautiful red bow sparkling with glitter. "I heard there was a party for friends and family," he said. Waited.

I took the present, and, on impulse, tippy-toed up to kiss his cheek.

"Friends and family are always welcome," I said, surprised to hear my voice had dropped a little, to feel the tingling zing inside as he smiled that slow and sexy smile of his, eyes sparkling.

I let him pass, entering the sitting room to place the gift he'd brought under the tree before returning to the foyer to watch him. He shook Dad's hand, Mom hugging him while he laughed and hugged her back. Which had my heart softening and my mind spinning over possibilities, wishes and hopes.

I couldn't help but wonder if maybe we might have a chance after all.

Christmas miracles, right?

Looking for more Fiona Fleming? There's another novella adventure now available! Go get your copy of **Birthday Wishes and Murder**, for sale now!

AUTHOR NOTES

My darling reader:

When I found myself, at the end of 2020, with a few extra days to fill before my two-week vacation (so excited!) I realized I had time for a fun project and, wouldn't you know, it was Fee who piped up first.

Told me she had a Christmas mystery to share and, within days of having that chat, I was wrapping up *Deck The Halls and Murder*, because that's how Fee rolls, yo.

She cracks me up.

I have one last project to finish before I take my holiday break. *Tropical Destinations and Death*, book six of the **Fleming Investigations Cozy Mysteries**, is waiting for me to start just as soon as I wrap up here (apparently Fee's Christmas puns are contagious...?). I'm looking forward to some time to rest, but already anticipating January's epic schedule.

I'll update you as I go but, for now, I wish you the very best, happiest, healthiest (!) and most delightful holiday season, no matter what you celebrate, with those you love close and safe. 2020 has been one of those years of turmoil and change we tend to look back on decades later with the rose-colored glasses of history.

Best to you, and Merry Christmas,
Patti

ABOUT THE AUTHOR

Everything you need to know about me is in this one statement: I've wanted to be a writer since I was a little girl, and now I'm doing it. How cool is that, being able to follow your dream and make it reality? I've tried everything from university to college, graduating the second with a journalism diploma (I sucked at telling real stories), am an enthusiastic improv performer (if you've never tried it, I highly recommend making things up as you go along as often as possible). I've even been in a Celtic girl band (some of our stuff is on YouTube!) and was an independent filmmaker (go check out the Lovely Witches Club). My life has been one creative thing after another—all leading me here, to writing books for a living.

Now with multiple series in happy publication, I live on beautiful and magical Prince Edward Island (I know you've heard of Anne of Green Gables) with my multitude of pets.

I love-love-love hearing from you! You can reach me (and I promise you, I'll always message back) at patti@pattilarsen.com. And if you're eager for your next dose of Patti Larsen books (usually about one release a month) come join my mailing list! All the best up and coming, giveaways, contests and, of course, my observations on the world (aren't you just dying to know what I think about everything?) all in one place: http://bit.ly/PattiLarsenEmail.

Last—but not least!—I hope you enjoyed what you read! Your happiness is my happiness. And I'd love to hear just what you thought. A review where you found this book would mean the world to me—reviews feed writers more than you will ever know. So, loved it (or not so much), your honest review would make my day. Thank you!